Johanna Spyri, Lucy Wheelock

Red-Letter Stories

Swiss tales from the German of Mad. Johanna Spyri

Johanna Spyri, Lucy Wheelock

Red-Letter Stories
Swiss tales from the German of Mad. Johanna Spyri

ISBN/EAN: 9783337299149

Printed in Europe, USA, Canada, Australia, Japan

Cover: Foto ©Andreas Hilbeck / pixelio.de

More available books at **www.hansebooks.com**

RED-LETTER STORIES

Swiss Tales

FROM THE GERMAN OF

MAD. JOHANNA SPYRI

BY

LUCY WHEELOCK

BOSTON

D. LOTHROP & CO., PUBLISHERS

FRANKLIN AND HAWLEY STREETS

TO THE

Little Children of Chauncy Hall Kindergarten,

WHO MAKE EVERY DAY A RED-LETTER DAY,

THESE LITTLE TALES

ARE

AFFECTIONATELY DEDICATED.

LUCY WHEELOCK.

CHAUNCY HALL SCHOOL,
    BOSTON, Nov. 1, 1884.

INTRODUCTORY NOTE.

THE Swiss tales in these volumes were written by Madame Johanna Spyri of Zurich, a writer of great popularity in her own country and Germany.

By some critics she is assigned the first place among German writers for children.

The "Revue Suisse" of August, 1882, says of her: "Since 1878 she has published a number of charming tales which children read and re-read, and which we, older people, *blasées* by romance of every kind, enjoy as the fruits of a lost paradise."

Madame Spyri authorizes this translation.

CONTENTS.

LISA'S CHRISTMAS.

BASTI'S SONG IN ALTORF.

RED-LETTER STORIES.

LISA'S CHRISTMAS.

CHAPTER I.

INTRODUCTION.

In a certain school there was a certain teacher, not more than fifty years ago, who had certain very unusual and charming ways of doing many things.

In the first place you must know her name. It was really Miss Sonnenschein; but, as that is a long name, and not easy to say, you may imagine the children were not long in changing it to Miss Sunshine. At last everybody had forgotten what her real name was, and she was called Miss Sunshine everywhere.

Among other pleasant things which Miss Sunshine did, one was this : —

Whenever all the children in her room had been very good and kind, and had worked very well, she put a big red letter on the black-board

7

at the end of the day, to show that it had been a red-letter day.

If you don't understand what a red-letter is, you must think of the very best day you ever had at the sea-shore, or in the country, and then you will know exactly what it is.

Miss Sunshine did not always make the same letter on the black-board. Sometimes it was an A; sometimes an E, or an H, or a K.

Nobody ever found out exactly what these letters meant; but the children suspected they had something to do with the child who had done the most to make a red-letter day, and each child would try to see if the letter belonged to his or her name. If it was A, Albert and Amy were glad; and if it was E, Elsie's face beamed with joy.

The best thing about these days was that then Miss Sunshine brought out her red-letter books. These were big story books marked with red letters, out of which most charming tales were read.

One winter, when the boys and girls had been studying about Switzerland, and had learned about its high mountains with their famous

passes, their snowy peaks, and glaciers, Miss
Sunshine took up a book with a big red S on
the cover, and said: "Now, I will read you
some stories about the little Swiss children, so
that you can see how the people live among the
Alps, and how the little people study and work
and play just as you do.

The first story is our Christmas story, and is
called "*Lisa's Christmas.*"

LISA'S CHRISTMAS.

The little village of Altkirch is situated
among beautiful green, willow-covered hills,
which encircle it completely, except on one
side, where one can look across to the green
Rechberg on whose summit stands another
village which, like the mountain, bears the
name of Rochberg. Between the two heights
rushes the wild Zillerbach. A zigzag road leads
down from Altkirch to the Zillerbach, across
the old covered bridge, and on the other side
zigzag again up to Rechberg, nearly two
miles in all. Shorter and much pleasanter is
the narrow foot-path, going directly down to the
Zillerbach, where a narrow wooden foot-bridge

spans the rushing stream. On all the green hills around, no human habitation is to be seen; but near the foot-path is a solitary chapel, which for many long years has looked down upon the rushing stream and the little foot-bridge, which has many a time fallen away and been renewed during these years.

There are many poor people in Altkirch, for there is little work. Most of the men go as day-laborers to the farms in the vicinity. A few possess a little spot of land which they cultivate.

At the time of our story one of the poorest households was that of Joseph of the Willow, who lived in a lonely old house on the way to the chapel, quite by itself. The little house was almost entirely covered by the long, over-hanging boughs of an old willow-tree, which had given to the owner the name of Joseph of the Willow. He had always lived in the little house, which had belonged to his father before him.

Now Joseph was an old man and had only an aged invalid wife and two grandchildren in the old house with him. His only son, Sepp, a

careless, good-natured young man, had been
away from them six years, and they did not
even know where he was. He had married,
early in life, an industrious young woman
named Constance, whom everybody liked. She
kept everything in the house in beautiful order,
and Joseph and his wife had a comfortable
time while she lived; she worked early and
late, and did not allow them to want for anything. " Father and mother must rest now,"
she said, " they have done enough, and we two
young people must make their last days pleasant." Sepp went every day to his work at the
great farm on the other side of the Zillerbach,
and brought home each week a nice sum of
money.

Three years passed by in undisturbed peace.

Old Father Clemens, who lived in the great
house behind Altkirch, said often, as he entered
Joseph's home, —

" Joseph, it is good to be with you; one never
hears an angry word here; all honor to your
good Constance." His kind eyes beamed with
joy when Constance bade him welcome with
her cheerful voice, and little Stanzeli stretched

out her tiny hands towards him. Then he said
again, "Yes, indeed, it is good to be here,
Joseph."

When Stanzeli was two years old, little Seppli came into the world.   That was a great joy
for everybody; but, soon after, the saddest thing
that could happen came to Joseph's home.

Constance was taken away from her husband
and from her children.   From that time Sepp
seemed like one who had no farther aim in life.
A restless, uneasy feeling took possession of
him.   He could no longer remain at home on
Sundays.   He spent more and more time away,
until he finally left them altogether.   For
a long time he sent home money for the support
of his children ; but at last this stopped, and for
six years nothing had been heard from him.

The two old people had grown poorer and
poorer, and more and more feeble.   Their only
support came from the baskets which the old
man wove from the willow-twigs and gave to
the dairyman when he took his cheese to the
city to market.   He did not earn much in this
way, and the closest economy was necessary to
make both ends meet.

Stanzeli was now nine years old and Seppli
seven. Stanzeli was the chief dependence of
the family, for her grandmother had been ill
now for more than four months. So she and
her grandfather had to do the cooking, which
was not very laborious, for there was nothing
to cook but meal porridge and potatoes, and
now and then a little coffee. But as Stanzeli
was too small to lift the kettle, and as Joseph
did not understand how to put things together,
the two were necessary in preparing a meal.

Seppli, too, assisted in the work by getting
first in the way of one and then of the other,
with eyes wide open in expectation of the wonderful porridge. It was useless to drive him
away, for he was back in two minutes.

One warm September day, when the sun was
shining on the green fields around Altkirch, and
some beams strayed through the dingy windows
to the grandmother's bed, the old woman sighed
and said: "Ah me! Does the sun shine still?
If I could only go out again! But I would be
willing to lie still if the bed were not as hard as
wood and the pillow not much better! And
when I think of the winter and the thin cover-

let — it makes me cold already—I shall certainly
freeze to death."

"Do n't worry now about the winter," said the
old man soothingly. "God will still be with
us. He has already helped us many times when
things looked dark. You must not forget that.
How would you like a little coffee to warm you
up?"

She thought she would like some very much,
so Joseph went into the next room, which was
the kitchen, to prepare it. He beckoned to
Stanzeli to come with him, and when he had
taken down the coffee-pot and poured some
water into it, he said, "Stanzeli, what comes
first?"

"I must grind the coffee beans," answered
the child, and, seating herself on the footstool
with the coffee-mill, she turned with all her
might. But something was wrong. She looked
here and there, and finally drew out the little
drawer.

There, instead of the fine powder which
should have been seen, lay great pieces as large
as half a coffee bean.

With a cry, Stanzeli showed the drawer to

her grandfather and pointed out the sad condition of things. He looked at the broken mill, and said quietly: "Don't make any noise that your grandmother can hear. It will make her unhappy, and she will think she can have no more coffee to drink. Just wait a little."

Thereupon he went out, and soon came back with a large stone in his hand, with which he pounded up the coffee kernels on a paper, and Stanzeli turned the coarsely pulverized mass into the pot. But as soon as the invalid took the little dish of coffee in her hand, she cried out complainingly: "Oh dear! Oh dear! Great grains of coffee are swimming about on the top; the coffee-mill is broken. Oh, if it only could have lasted! We are not able to buy a new one."

"Don't make yourself ill over it," said Joseph in a soothing tone. "Many things are brought about by patience."

"Yes," said his wife; "but no coffee-mill."

A little cup of the coffee was given to the children with their potato; for they had bread only on Sunday.

Then Joseph found some baskets which were

finished, and, binding them together in pairs;
gave them to the children, and told them to
set out at once, that they might get home in
good season. They knew well where they had
to go, for every two weeks they were sent on
such an errand to the dairyman. He lived
quite a distance from the little village. The
way led over the hill, past the chapel, up to the
forest, where his cottage stood.

The children started out together, and, since
Stanzeli kept conscientiously on the way, Seppli
had to do the same, although he would have
preferred to stand still and look at this or that.

When they came to the chapel, Stanzeli
paused for the first time and said: "Lay the
baskets here on the ground, Seppli; we must go
into the chapel and say '*Our Father.*'"

But Seppli was unwilling to go. "I do not
wish to go in, it is too warm," he said, and
seated himself on the ground.

"No, Seppli, come, we must do it," said Stanzeli. "Don't you remember that Father
Clemens said that when one passed a church
one must always go in and pray? Get up and
come quickly."

Seppli remained stubborn; but his sister gave him no rest. She took him by the hand and drew him up.

"You must come, Seppli. You are not doing right. One ought to pray willingly."

At that moment they heard steps coming up towards the chapel, and Father Clemens suddenly stood before the children. Seppli sprang quickly to his feet, and both children offered him their hands.

"Seppli, Seppli!" he said kindly, as he pressed his hand, "what have I heard? Are you not willing to follow Stanzeli when she wishes to go into the chapel? I wish to tell you something: our Heavenly Father does not command us to go into the church and pray; but He gives us the privilege of doing so, and every time we pray He sends us something, only we cannot always see it immediately."

The good man went on his way, and Seppli went into the chapel without further objection. When they came out again a few minutes later they heard the sound of voices coming from the foot-path which leads down to the Zillerbach.

Three heads appeared, one after the other, and at last three children, two boys and a girl, came into full view, who stared at the other two in astonishment.

CHAPTER II.

THE largest of these children, who appeared
so unexpectedly, was the girl, who might have
been eleven years old. One of her brothers
was a year younger, perhaps, and the other was
much younger and smaller, but very fat and
firmly built.

The little girl moved a few steps nearer
Stanzeli and Seppli, and asked, —

" What are your names? "

The children gave their names.

" Where do you live? " was the next question.

" In Altkirch, there, you can see the church
tower from here," answered Stanzeli, pointing
to the red tower between the hills.

"So you have your church there. We have
such a church, too ; but it is closed, and we go
into it only on Sunday. But we have no such

19

chapels with us. There is another still higher above us; only look, Kurt, up by the forest."

The little girl pointed with her finger high above, and her brother nodded to indicate that he saw the designated object. "I should like to know why you have so many chapels here on all the hills."

"So that we can go in and pray when we are passing by," said Stanzeli quickly.

"We can do that without them," responded the other girl, "we can pray everywhere, where-ever we are. God hears everywhere; that I know."

"Yes but we might not think of it, unless we came to a chapel; then we should be reminded," answered Stanzeli.

"We must go now, Lisa," said her brother Kurt, to whom the conversation was becoming tiresome. But Lisa was enjoying it. She liked Stanzeli because she answered so decidedly and had given her something to think about.

All at once the chapel made a different im-pression upon her. Until now she had looked upon it simply as a building which is left stand-ing because it was put there a long time ago.

Now it seemed to her as if God pointed down from heaven to the chapel and said, " There it stands, that you may think of me."

As Lisa, following her own train of thought, did not speak for some time, Stanzeli continued : "And we are not commanded to go in and pray, but are permitted to do so. And then God always sends us something, even if we are not able to see it. Father Clemens has said so."

" Yes; but I would rather have something we can see," interposed Seppli, who had been listening attentively.

" Do you know Father Clemens, too ? " asked Lisa eagerly, for he was well-known to all the children on the other side of the Zillerbach too. Wherever he was seen in his long coat with the great crucifix at his side, the children ran to him, offering their hands eagerly. He always had his pockets full of beautiful picture cards for them. Lisa had received many of these, so the name of Father Clemens recalled to her mind the pleasantest recollections.

" He lives in Altkirch, up in the old convent, and he comes often to see us," exclaimed Stanzeli. " Yes, and he sometimes brings grandmother a whole loaf of bread," added Seppli, who remembered this good act most vividly.

"I must go now," said Stanzeli, as she took up her baskets. "We have still a long way to go."

"Won't you come some time to Rechberg to see me?" asked Lisa, who wanted to continue the acquaintance.

"I don't know the way. I have never been on the other side of the Zillerbach."

"Oh, it is very easy to find. Just cross the foot-bridge, then up and up until you come to the top. That is Rechberg. The large house which stands highest of all is ours. Do come soon. Come early some afternoon, so that we can play till evening."

So the children separated. Stanzeli and Seppli went on up the mountain, and Lisa looked about for her brothers, who had disappeared.

Kurt had climbed up an old pine-tree near the chapel, and was rocking on a bough, which cracked in a most ominous manner. Lisa watched to see him come down, considering that event more amusing than dangerous.

Karl was lying on the ground near the pine-tree, sound asleep.

Something came running down the hill, which brought Kurt from his lofty perch, and woke Karl from his sleep at once. It was a flock of sheep, young and old, great and small, all skipping, running, and bleating, while the great dog barked continually. The shepherd was driving them towards Altkirch. The three children looked at the flock as it went by, in silent admiration. As far as they could see, they watched the young lambs skipping along by the sober mothers. When they had all passed, Karl said with a deep sigh; "If only we had a lamb like one of those!"

That was exactly what Kurt and Lisa thought at the same moment, and for once the three agreed perfectly.

Lisa immediately proposed that they should go home, and beg and beg for a lamb until they got it. She pictured to her brothers how they could take the lamb everywhere with them, and play with it in the pasture, until all three became so excited over the prospect, that they finally ran down the mountain and over the foot-bridge. Lisa went first, followed by Kurt, and they rushed so fast that the bridge swayed under their feet, and the loose boards moved up and down in such a manner that Karl, who was behind them, lost his footing, and almost fell into the rushing Zillerbach. Kurt turned and helped him up, and they finally reached the other side in safety.

It was a long way to Rechberg, and the lights had been brought into the sitting-room when the children came in sight of the house. Their mother had been anxiously watching for them for more than an hour. She had seen nothing of them since dinner, and they should have been at home for four-o'clock coffee. She had given them permission to spend their afternoon in the grove near by, of which they had availed themselves most joyfully.

Now it was dark; and there was no sight or sound of them. How could they be so late? She conjured up all possible accidents, and ran from window to window, more and more anxious.

But now — ah! there were their voices! They came nearer! She ran out — yes — there they

were coming up the mountain-side. As they
saw their mother they ran faster, each trying to
be the first to tell the story. Little Karl was
left behind, but Kurt and Lisa came up breath-
less, eager to begin their tale at once.

At the same time a strong voice came from
the opposite direction; "Supper! supper!"

It was the bailiff's, who had just returned
from his business and wished to enforce the
strict order of his household. When they were
all seated at the supper table, the children were
permitted to give an account of their day's
adventures.

It seemed that Lisa had grown tired of the
grove, and had proposed to climb up to the old
linden, where there was a fine view of the
chapel, and the Zillerbach with its narrow
bridge. Lisa had had a previous experience of
the trembling and swaying of the little bridge,
and an irresistible desire had seized her to visit
the vicinity again.

Her brothers were very willing to join her,
and the walk was begun which proved a much
longer one than they had anticipated. They
recounted the events of their expedition again

and again, the meeting with the two children, seeing the flock of sheep, and crossing the shaky bridge.

The consequence of this last account was that all expeditions to the Zillerbach were strictly forbidden for the future.

In the meantime little Karl had fallen fast asleep in his chair.

"See, Karl is resting after his day's work," said their father, "and it is high time for yours to be at an end."

It was not easy to waken the little sleeper, so the bailiff took him, chair and all, and carried him into the chamber, while the other children followed, laughing and shouting at the funny sight.

From that time, at every meal, morning, noon, and night, one after the other, the children would say:

"Oh, if only we had a lamb!"

One evening, when the mother and children were sitting around the table, and little Karl, who found the school-work of the others rather tiresome, had said for the sixth time: "Oh, if we only had a lamb!" the door opened suddenly and in sprang a real live lamb. The little creature was covered with snow-white curly wool and was prettier than any the children had ever seen.

Such a cry of joy, such a noise arose, that nobody could hear a word.

The lamb darted from one corner to another in fright, bleating pitifully, while the children rushed after him with shouts of joy.

At last their father called : " Come, that's enough. We must take the lamb to his new quarters, and then I have something to say to you."

The children went out to see where the lamb was put, full of wonder as to the place. A little addition had been made to the stable, and nice, clean straw lay on the floor for the lamb's bed. There was a little manger, too, in which to put grass and hay for him.

When the pretty creature had been carefully placed on his straw bed and was quiet, the father closed the low door and motioned to the children to follow him. When they had returned to the sitting-room, he said seriously: " Now listen to me, and give heed to what I

say. I have taken the lamb away from his
mother to give to you. You must take the
mother's place and care for him, so he will not
die of home-sickness. You may take him out
with you during your play-time wherever you
wish; but you must never leave him alone, and,
whoever takes him out must take care of him
and bring him back to 'his place. Do you
understand, and are you willing to care for him
in this way? If not, I will take him back to his
mother."

All three, Lisa, Kurt, and Karl, begged their
father to leave the lamb with them, and promised faithfully to obey his commands in every
respect, and were so full of joy at the prospect
of having a real live lamb that they could not
easily get to sleep that night. Even little Karl,
usually so sleepy, sat up in bed and called out,
again and again:

"Papa shall see that the lamb will not die
here. I will take care of that."

Sometimes they went to the pasture.

CHAPTER III.

THE EFFECT OF CONCEALMENT.

THE next day the great question was what the lamb's name would be.

Liza proposed calling it " *Eulalia*," for that was the name of her friend's cat, and it seemed to her an especially fine name. But the boys did not like it. It was too long. Kurt proposed " Nero," as the big dog at the mill was called. But Lisa and Karl were not pleased with this name.

In despair, they went to their mother, who suggested he should be called " Curlyhead," and Curlyhead he was from that time forth.

The little creature soon became a great pet for the children. They took him out for a frolic whenever they had a few spare moments. Sometimes they went to the pasture, and Kurt and Karl would search for rich, juicy clover-leaves to bring him, while Lisa sat on a bank with the little creature's head in her lap.

Whenever a child was sent on an errand to the mill, or to the baker's, the lamb must go, and he listened so intelligently to all the conversation his companion addressed to him that it was evident he understood every word. He grew every day more trustful, and thrived so well under this excellent care that he grew round as a ball, and his wool was as white and pretty as if he were always in his Sunday dress.

The beautiful, sunny autumn was drawing to an end, and November came. Christmas was coming, and every child's mind was filled with expectations of that joyful event. Kurt and Karl disclosed all their cherished dreams to Curlyhead, and assured him he should have his share of holiday presents. Curlyhead listened attentively and seemed to appreciate these confidences.

Lisa had a particular friend, Marie, who lived in the great farmhouse on the way to the Zillerbach. Lisa was very anxious to visit this friend, for she could talk over her prospects for Christmas more fully with her than with her brothers. She had permission to go on her first free afternoon, and when the time came she was so impatient to start that she could hardly hold still long enough for her mother to tie on her warm scarf. Then she ran bounding off, while her mother watched her until she was half-way down the hill; then she turned and went into the house again.

At that moment it came into Lisa's mind that Curlyhead would enliven the long way if her brothers had not already taken him. She quickly turned around, ran back to the barn, and took out Curlyhead. Together they ran down the hard path where the bright autumn leaves were dancing about in the wind. They soon reached the end of their journey, where Lisa and her friend were quickly lost in deep conversation, walking up and down on the sunny plot of ground in front of the house, while Curlyhead nibbled contentedly at the hedge.

The two friends refreshed themselves occasionally with pears, and juicy, red apples, which grew in great abundance on the farm.

Marie's mother had brought out a great basketful, and Lisa was to carry home what were left. When it was time for Lisa to go

home, Marie accompanied her a little way, and
they still had so much to say, that they were in
sight of Lisa's home before they knew it. Marie
quickly took leave of her, and Lisa hurried
up the path. It was already dark. Just as
she reached the house, the thought flashed
through her mind like lightning: "Where is
Curlyhead?"

She knew she had taken him with her. She
had seen him nibbling the hedge, and then she
had entirely forgotten him.

In a most dreadful fright she rushed back
down the mountain again, calling, " Curlyhead,
Curlyhead, where are you? Oh, come, come!"

But all was still. Curlyhead was nowhere to
be seen. Lisa ran back to the farmhouse. There
was a light already in the window of the sitting-
room, and she could look in from the stone steps
by the house. They were all at the supper-table;
father, mother, Marie, and her brothers and the
servants. The old cat lay on a bench by the
stove; but nowhere was there a trace of Curlyhead to be seen, as Lisa peered into all the
corners. Then she ran around the house into
the garden, around the hedge, again into the

garden, and along the inside of the hedge, calling, " Curlyhead, come now, oh, come, come ! "

All in vain. There was no sight or sound of the lamb. Lisa grew more anxious. It grew darker and the wind howled louder and louder, and almost blew her from the ground.

She must go home. What should she do? She did not dare to say she had lost Curlyhead. If she could see her mother alone, first!

She ran as fast as she could up the mountain. At home supper was ready, and her father was already there. She burst into the room in such a heated, disordered condition, that her mother said : " You cannot come to the table so, child ; go and make yourself ready first." And her father added : " You must not come home so late ! Now go, and come soon in a neater condition, or you will have nothing to eat."

Lisa obeyed quietly. As far as supper was concerned, it was all the same to her ; she would much rather not come in at all ; but that would not do. With a very sad face she returned to her place. She had a fearful anxiety in regard to the remarks and questions sure to follow,

But before any one could say anything to her, a new occurrence claimed the attention of the whole family.

Hans put his head in at the door and said: " Excuse me, sir, but Trina says the children are all at home and the lamb is not yet in the barn."

" What?" cried the bailiff. " What can this mean? Who has taken him out?"

" Not I!" " Not I! Certainly not I!" " Nor I," cried out Kurt and Karl so loudly that one could not hear whether Lisa spoke or not.

" Not so fast," said their mother gently. " It certainly was not Lisa, she went alone this afternoon to visit Marie, and has only just come back."

" Then it is one of you boys," cried their father hastily, looking sharply at the two brothers.

A great cry came as answer, " Not I!" " Not I!" and both of them looked so honest that the bailiff said at once: " No! No! It is not you; Hans must have left the door open an instant, and the lamb took the opportunity of running out. I must look into it."

He left the room hastily to make an examination of the barn.

When the first excitement was over another idea became uppermost. All at once Karl covered his eyes with his hands, and sobbed out, —

" Now Curlyhead is lost. We shall never see him any more. Perhaps he is already dead."

And Kurt added, weeping aloud: "Yes, it grows colder, and he has nothing to eat and will surely freeze and die in misery."

Lisa began to cry more violently than her brothers. She said nothing, but one could easily see how much deeper her grief was than theirs, and Lisa herself knew why. Long after Kurt and Karl were asleep, dreaming happy dreams of Curlyhead, Lisa lay tossing uneasily, and could not sleep. Besides her grief for the lamb left to wander alone.in the cold night, she had to bear the torture of the thought that she was the cause of this, and that she had concealed it when she ought to have confessed it. She had not, it is true, called out " Not I, not I;" but she had been silent when her mother said: " It certainly cannot be Lisa," and she rightly felt that by her silence she had done the same wrong as if she had told an untruth. She could not rest until she determined to tell her mother the whole story in the morning. Perhaps he would be found.

The next morning was bright and sunny, and at breakfast it was decided that, as soon as school was out, all three children should go out to look for Curlyhead. In the afternoon they would do the same. He must be somewhere, and they would find him. Their mother told them, too, that their father had already, in the early morning, sent Hans out to search for the little creature everywhere; so there was every hope that he would be found. Lisa was most happy at this prospect, and thought she would not need to say anything now; everything would come right. The whole Rechberg was searched during the day, and inquiries made in every house; but Curlyhead seemed to have disappeared from the face of the earth. Nobody had seen him, and nowhere was there any trace of him. The search was continued for several days; but in vain. Then the bailiff said it was of no use: either the poor animal

And one looked here, and one there at the window.

was no longer alive, or it had wandered far away.

A few days after, the first snow fell, and so thick and large were the flakes that in a short time the whole garden lay in deep snow, which came half way up the hedge. Generally, the children rejoiced greatly in the first snow; and the more the flakes whirled about, the more they shouted and exulted.

Now they were quiet, and one looked here, and one there, at the window, and each one thought in silence of Curlyhead, wondering if he lay under the cold snow or was trying to wade through it and could not, and was calling for help with his well-known voice, and no one was near to hear. When their father came home at night, he said : "It is a bitterly cold night ; the snow is already frozen hard. If the poor animal is not already dead, it will certainly perish to-night. Would that I had never brought the poor creature home!" Then Karl broke out in such bitter weeping, and Kurt and Lisa joined in such a heartrending manner, that their father left the room, and their mother sought to comfort them.

From that time the bailiff never mentioned
the lamb again, and when the children grieved
for it, their mother talked to them about the
Christmas celebration. She told them that the
Christ-child came to make all hearts glad, and
that this festival, which would soon come, would
make them happy again. And when tender-
hearted Karl began, as the cold, dark evenings
came on to say despondingly: " Oh, if only Curlyhead were not freezing in the cold outside ! "
Then his mother comforted him, by saying:
" See, Karl, the good God takes care of animals,
too. It may be that he has prepared a warm bed
for Curlyhead elsewhere, and it is well with him ;
and since we can care no more for him, let us be
content and leave him with the good God."
Kurt listened attentively as their mother comforted Karl, and so it happened that, gradually,
the two brothers became happy again, and rejoiced more every day in the prospect of the
pleasant Christmas time. But Lisa did not
grow cheerful with them. A heavy burden lay
upon her, which crushed her down and kept her
always unhappy. At night she dreamed of
seeing Curlyhead lying out in the snow, hungry

and freezing, looking at her with reproachful eyes which said, "You have done it." Then she would wake up weeping, and afterwards, when she tried to be merry with her brothers, she could not, for she always kept thinking, If they knew what she had done, how they would reproach her! She dared not look straight in the eyes of her parents, for she had concealed from them what she ought to have revealed, and now she could not bring the words to her lips; she had let them believe so long that she knew nothing about the affair.

So Lisa had no more happy minutes, and every day she appeared more mournful and full of grief; and when Kurt and Karl came to her and said: "Do be happy, Lisa; Christmas is coming, and only think of what may happen," then the tears came to her eyes, and, half weeping, she said, "I can never be happy, no, never, not even at Christmas."

That grieved tender-hearted Karl, and he said comfortingly: "Do you know, Lisa, when we can do nothing more, then we must leave all to God, and then we are happy again if we have done nothing wrong? Mamma said so." Lisa, then, began to cry in earnest, so that it alarmed Karl, and he ran away, as Kurt had already done. Lisa's altered demeanor had not escaped her mother's notice. She often watched the child in silence, but asked her no questions.

CHAPTER IV.

A GIFT.

NOVEMBER came to an end. The snow had become deeper, and every day the cold grew more bitter. Stanzeli's grandmother in Alt-kirch moved her thin coverlet here and there, and could hardly keep warm under it. The room was cold, too, for their supply of wood was very scanty, and with the deep snow there were no sticks to be found. Coffee was very rarely made, and it had to be ground with stones, as the mill was useless, and there was no money for a new one. The poor grandmother had many things to complain of. Her husband sat, most of the time, by the stove, seeking to soothe her, and weaving at the same time his little willow baskets.

It had snowed for so long, and the deep snow was so soft, that the old man had been obliged to take his baskets to the dairyman himself, for

the children would have been buried in the
snow. No path had been made up the mountain, so that even the grandfather had trouble
in getting through. But at last the sky was
clear, and the high fields of snow, far and wide,
were frozen so hard that one could go over them
as over a firm street; the ice did not crack under the heaviest man.

Now the children could be sent out again.
Stanzeli wound a shawl about her, Seppli put
on his woollen cap, and they started out, each
with a bundle of baskets. As they came to the
chapel in about half an hour, Stanzeli laid her
baskets down, and took Seppli by the hand to
go in. But Seppli was obstinate again. "I will
not go in. I do not wish to pray. My fingers
are freezing," he said, and planted his feet
on the ground so that Stanzeli could not move
him.

But she begged and entreated, and reminded
him of what Father Clemens had said, and was
very anxious, for Seppli might bring them both
a great good. Stanzeli had heard and understood so much of grief and misery that it
seemed to her a great happiness and comfort to

kneel down and pray to a Father in heaven
who will help all poor people. Seppli finally
gave up, and they entered the quiet chapel.
Stanzeli said her prayer softly and thoughtfully.
All at once a peculiar cry sounded through the
stillness. Stanzeli was a little frightened, and
turned to Seppli, saying softly, "Don't do so in
the chapel; you must be still." Seppli replied
just as softly, but indignantly, "I don't do it;
it is you."

A that moment the cry sounded again, and
louder. Seppli looked carefully at a place in
the rear of the church by the altar. Suddenly
he touched Stanzeli's arm and drew her so
forcibly from her seat towards the altar, that she
could do nothing but follow. Here, at the foot
of the altar, half covered by the altar cloth under
which it crouched, lay a white lamb, trembling
and shaking with the cold, and stretching out its
thin legs as if it could move no more from
weariness.

"It is a lamb; now we have something given
to us that we can see," exclaimed Seppli in de-
light.

Stanzeli looked in great astonishment at the

little animal. Father Clemens's words had come into her mind also, and she believed nothing else than that God, who gives something to everyone who prays, had sent the lamb to them to-day. Only she could not understand how the little creature seemed so weary, and lay as if half dead. Even her caresses failed to arouse the poor lamb.

" We will take him home with us and give him a potato," said Seppli, who knew no other cause of misery than hunger.

" What are you thinking of, Seppli? We must go to the dairyman's," said faithful Stanzeli; " but we cannot leave the little thing here alone," and the child looked thoughtfully at the poor creature with its troubled breathing.

" I know, now," she continued, after some reflection. " You take care of the lamb, here, and I will run up with the baskets as fast as I can, and come back for you."

Seppli was pleased with the proposition, and Stanzeli ran on immediately. She darted over the fields of snow as nimbly as a deer. Seppli seated himself on the floor and looked at his present. The lamb was covered with such

beautiful thick wool, that he took great pleasure
in burying his hand in it, and it became at once
so beautifully warm that he quickly thrust in
the other also. He drew very near to the little
creature, and it was like a small stove for him;
for although it trembled with the cold itself, yet
its woolly covering afforded an excellent means
of warmth to Seppli. In less than half an hour
Stanzeli came back, and now they wished to take
their gift home to their grandparents. But in
vain did they try to place the lamb on its feet;
it was so feeble that it fell down at once with a
mournful cry, when they had raised it a little.

"It must be carried," said Stanzeli; "but it is
too heavy for me, you must help me;" and she
showed Seppli how he must take hold so as not
to hurt the lamb, and they carried it away together. Their progress was a little slow, for
it was quite inconvenient for the two to go
far with their load; but they were so delighted
that they did not give up until they reached
their cottage, and could rush in with their new-
found treasure.

"We have a sheep; a live sheep with very
warm wool," cried Seppli, as he entered; and

when they were inside the room, they laid the
lamb on the seat near the stove, by their astonished grandfather.   Then Stanzeli told how
everything had happened, and how it had come
exactly as Father Clemens had said: that God
sends something whenever one prays; only it
cannot always be seen at once.

"But to-day we can see it," interposed Seppli
joyfully.

Joseph looked at his wife to see what she
thought, and she looked at him, saying, "you
must tell them, Joseph."

After some reflection he said, "Somebody must
go up to Father Clemens, and ask him how
we are to understand that.   I will go myself."
With that he rose from his seat, put on his old
fur cap, and went out.

Father Clemens came back with him.

When he had greeted the invalid, he sat down
and looked carefully at the poor, exhausted
lamb.   Then he drew the children to him and
said kindly; "This is how it is: when we pray,
God gives us cheerful and courageous hearts,
and that is a beautiful gift on which many
others depend.   This lamb is lost; it must be-

long to the large flock which passed through late in the autumn, and the shepherd will certainly enquire for it. It must have been lost a long time, for it is nearly starved and almost dead; perhaps we cannot bring it back to life. First it must have a little warm milk, and then we can see what more it can take."

With the last words the good Father had lifted the lamb a little and laid his hand tenderly under its head.

Joseph said faintly, " We will do what we can. Stanzeli, go and see if there is a drop of milk."

But Father Clemens prevented Stanzeli from going and said; " I do not mean that; if it is agreeable to you, I will take the lamb. I have room and can take care of it."

That was a great relief to the old people, for they did not wish to leave the lamb to die of hunger, and 'where there was anything to feed it they did not know.

So Father Clemens took the tired animal on his arm, and went with it to the old cloister. For a long time Seppli looked after him and grumbled a little,

A few days after, the grandfather saw Father Clemens coming again to their house, and said to the grandmother, in astonishment, "What does it mean; why is the good Father coming so soon again?"

"The lamb is probably dead, and he wishes to tell us, so that we may not expect in vain a reward from the shepherd for finding it."

Father Clemens entered; one could see that he had no pleasant message to bring. Stanzeli and Seppli sprang quickly towards him to offer him their hands.

He caressed them kindly, then said in a low tone to the grandfather, "it would be well to send the children away for a while; I have something to say to you."

The grandfather became a little uneasy, and thought to himself, "If I could only put mother out of the way, so that she would not hear if there is anything disagreeable to be related."

He gave Stanzeli the tin can and said, "Go with Seppli and get the milk, and if it is a little too early you can wait at the farm; it is warm in the cow-shed."

When the children were gone, Father Clemens moved his chair nearer to the bed and said, "Come a little nearer, Joseph ; I must disclose something to you. I do it unwillingly, however. Sepp has disgraced himself somewhat."

Hardly were these words spoken when the grandmother raised a fearful lamentation, and cried again and again, "Oh, my God, that I must pass through this! It was my last hope that Sepp would sometime reform and come home and help us in our last days, and now all that is past. Perhaps we must bear a great shame, and we have kept ourselves honorable and honest to a good old age. How willingly I would lie on my hard bed without complaining, and with never a good taste of coffee, if only this were not true! Oh, if he had not brought us to misfortune and shame!"

The old man sat affrighted and thunderstruck. "What has he done, Father," he asked, hesitatingly; "is it a wicked deed?"

Father Clemens answered that he did not know at all what it was; he had only understood that Sepp had done something over on the other side of the Zillerbach, for which he must answer to the bailiff on the Rechberg, who would certainly have him imprisoned.

"Alas, has he done it over there?" broke out the grandmother anew, "Ah, how will it go with him? They will certainly punish him severely enough, because he is of another faith."

"No, no, you must not take it so, grandmother," said Father Clemens deprecatingly; "it is not so. The bailiff is not unjust, and he is right-minded as far as belief is concerned. I have heard him say more than once; 'A virtuous and God-fearing man on this side of the Zillerbach, and such a one on the other side, both pray to the same Father in Heaven, and the prayer of one is just as precious to Him as the prayer of the other!' I have known the bailiff for many years, and I can tell you that I have had edifying conversations with him and his wife hundreds of times, and we have understood each other so well that it has done us good, and I feel a real inclination to go again when I have not been there for a long time. I have it now in my mind to go there soon to see how it stands with Sepp, and to speak a good word for him to the bailiff."

The old people were very glad and grateful

for this proposal. But her distress prompted the grandmother to say once more, complainingly, "If I only did not have to blame myself! I have brought this on us because I have lamented and complained so much over our narrow means. I will do it no more, I will be patient. Do you think our Father in Heaven will accept my repentance, and not punish me so severely?"

Father Clemens comforted her, and advised her to keep her good resolution.

Then he arose and promised her to come again as soon as he had been to the Rechberg, to bring news of Sepp.

Joseph accompanied the priest outside the house, and then asked, " How is the lamb? Is it still living, or has it perished?"

"No signs of perishing," answered Father Clemens cheerfully, "it is round and fat and plays merrily again, and it is such a trustful little creature that I shall be sorry to give it up when the shepherd comes. I have sent him word that the lamb is with me, so he will probably leave it until he comes to this region again ; and now, God be with you."

He shook Joseph's hand and went quickly away, for he had other sick ones to comfort who waited longingly for him; for in all Altkirch and far beyond, Father Clemens was the comforter for the poor and sick.

CHAPTER V.

THE long-desired Christmas Day had come at last. Kurt and Karl had been in a fever of expectation all day, and wandered restlessly from one room to another, unable to keep still anywhere. They had the feeling that they might bring the evening more quickly by constant motion.

Lisa sat quietly in a corner, and gave no attention to what her brothers were saying. She had never known such a Christmas. A heavy burden lay upon her, which stifled every feeling of joy. When she tried to force herself to throw off this weight and to be merry with her brothers, she found it impossible. She fancied all the time she heard some one coming who had found Curlyhead dead, and who would tell her father that it was she who had forgotten and left him.

53

Towards evening Kurt and Karl found a moment's rest, and sat together in a state of listening expectation, talking in subdued whispers.

" What should you think of a croquet game with colored balls? " whispered Karl. " Do you suppose the Christ-child thinks of that? "

" Perhaps," answered Kurt; " but do you know, I would much rather have a new sled; for you see *Kessler* does not run well, and we have only *Geiss* besides. When Lisa feels like playing again, she will want to coast, and then she will have *Geiss* and there is not room for us both on *Kessler*."

" Yes. But then there are the soldiers. Don't you know how many thousand times we have wished for a set of soldiers? " said Karl. " I would almost rather go without the sled than the soldiers."

" Perhaps," said Kurt slowly, for a new thought had already come to him.

" But suppose the Christ-child should bring a paint-box, then we could paint those pictures of soldiers, and make our own."

"Oh! Oh!" ejaculated Karl, quite taken by the charming prospect.

Just then their mother entered the room, and said, "Children, the candles are lit on the piano and we will go and sing. Where is Lisa?"

In the twilight, she had not noticed that Lisa was sitting in the corner of the room, neither had her brothers known she was there. She came out now and went to the piano with the others. Her mother seated herself and played for them to sing. Kurt and Karl sang lustily and Lisa joined in softly.

When they came to the words in the song: "*Jesus is greater, Jesus is greater, He who rejoices our sad hearts,*" Karl sang them so joyfully and loudly that one could see he did not have a sad heart. But Lisa had known what it was to have a sad heart; she swallowed a lump in her throat, and could not sing any more.

When the song was ended, their mother rose and said: "Now stay here quietly until I come again." But Lisa ran after her and said mournfully,—

"Mamma! Mamma! may I ask you something?"

The mother drew the child into her sleeping-room and asked her what she wanted.

"Mamma, can Jesus make all sad hearts happy again?" asked Lisa anxiously. "Yes, child, all," answered the mother, "all, whatever burdens them. Only one He cannot make happy, and that is one which holds a wrong and will not lay it aside."

Lisa broke out into loud crying. "I will hold it no longer," she sobbed. "I will tell it. I took Curlyhead away with me and forgot him, and lost him, and then I was silent, and I am the cause of his starving and freezing, and I cannot rejoice any more, not over anything."

Her mother drew Lisa lovingly to her, and said comfortingly,—

"Now you have experienced, my child, how a wrong deed hidden in our hearts can make us terribly unhappy. You will think of it, and never wish to do it again. But now you have confessed it repentantly; and the holy Christ can and will come into your heart, and make it happy again, for to-day He wishes especially to make all hearts glad. Now dry your tears and go to your brothers. I will come soon."

Such a weight had been taken from Lisa's heart, and she felt all at once so light and free, that she could almost have jumped over all the mountains.

Suddenly the thought came to her — to-day is Christmas! Anything may happen to-day! Everything within her rejoiced. There was only one shadow — Curlyhead! Where was he now?

As she went skipping towards her brothers, Karl said gladly, "I knew Lisa would be merry again at Christmas."

While Lisa was talking very fast about what she expected and hoped for, the house-bell sounded, loud and long, and Karl, pale with excitement, cried, " The Christ-child!"

At that moment their mother opened the door, and a flood of light streamed in from the next room. The children rushed in. There was such a blaze and sparkle and splendor that at first they could distinguish nothing.

Ah! Yes; in the middle of the room was a great pine-tree, gleaming with candles from top to bottom, covered with beautiful angels, brilliant birds, red strawberries and cherries, and golden apples and pears.

The children ran around the tree in speechless admiration. Suddenly, something came running in which almost knocked Lisa down. She uttered a shout of joy. Surely — it was — Curlyhead!

Round as a ball, and pretty as ever, he came and rubbed his head good-naturedly against Lisa's dress, bleating for joy. Kurt and Karl could hardly believe their eyes. Not hungry, not cold, — alive and well! it was really Curlyhead. They almost smothered him in their joy. But Karl had seen something else. He made a dive towards the table.

"Kurt! Kurt!" he cried, almost beside himself, "the soldiers! the soldiers!"

But Kurt had already darted to the other side and called back: "Come here! Here is the new sled, a splendid sled!"

As Karl ran towards him he cried again: "Oh, here is the paint-box! Only see how many brushes."

Lisa still hugged Curlyhead. He was her

best present. Now she could be perfectly
happy again. Everything was right.

Suddenly she saw two great eyes staring in
wonder at the splendid tree. They belonged to
Seppli, and there was Stanzeli standing near
him.

Lisa went to the children.

"So you have come at last to see me?" she
said. "Isn't the tree beautiful? Did you
know the Christ-child would come to-day?"

"Oh, no," said Stanzeli shyly. "Your
mother brought us here. Father Clemens told
us to-day that the lamb belonged to you, and
that we might bring it over."

"And you brought Curlyhead? Where from?
Where did you find it? How can he look so
fat and well?"

"You will know all that some other time,
Lisa," said her mother, coming towards the
children. "Now you must lead your little
friends to their Christmas table by the window. The Christ-child has remembered them,
too."

At first, nothing could induce Seppli to move
from the wonderful tree. Such a gleaming,

splendid thing he had never seen in all his life. He could not take his eyes off it.

At last Lisa said: "Do come, Seppli. You can see the tree just as well by the table, and then you can find out what the Christ-child has brought to you."

Seppli moved slowly away, without taking his eyes from the tree. But when he looked at the table, there was another pleasant sight. In the centre was the largest loaf of cake he had ever seen, flanked by apples and nuts. Near by was a school-bag, with books, a slate, and pencils. There was a thick, warm jacket, such as he never had in his life. When Lisa said: "These are Seppli's," he stood, as if glued to the spot, and could hardly believe it.

He looked first at Stanzeli, and then at his treasure, but Stanzeli was busy with her own presents, a beautiful new dress, and a handsome work-box.

She was much frightened when the bailiff came straight towards her, with a strange man who had been standing in the door with Hans and Trina.

"You would hardly know them now," said the bailiff, turning away again.

The man put out his hand.

" Give me your hand, Stanzeli," he said. The child obeyed, looking at him doubtfully.

" Stanzeli. Stanzeli," cried the stranger, much moved, " Don't look at me so. I am your father; do say one word to me. Your eyes are so like your mother's," and he wiped his eyes as he spoke.

" We have nobody but grandfather and grandmother," said Seppli decidedly, who had heard everything.

" No, Seppli. You have a father, too, and I am he," said the man, taking each of the children by the hand. " You must learn to know me, Stanzeli. You will be kind to your father, will you not? You have grown just like your mother," and the man wiped his eyes again.

" Yes, I will, indeed," said Stanzeli. " But I do not know you."

The bailiff, who had been watching them, now came nearer. " Sepp," he said gravely, " I know another father and mother whom it grieves that their child does not know them, and has no grateful service for them. But it is Christmas to-day, and we must all be merry. Go and

harness Brownie into the sleigh now, and
drive your children home. I leave the rest to
you."

" May God reward you a thousandfold," said
Sepp gratefully. " You shall be satisfied with
me, as surely as I wish God to have mercy on
my poor soul."

" Right. Now be off, Sepp. This goes in the
sleigh," said the bailiff, pointing to a large roll
near the children's table. Sepp took it on his
shoulders and went off.

The children's presents were soon packed up,
and they took their leave, promising to come
again on the first fine Sunday.

Then Trina put the children in the sleigh,
and Lisa's mother called to her :

" Wrap them up well in the robe, Trina, so
that they will not be cold."

Then the merry-making went on inside,
around the Christmas-tree, where all the presents were admired, and Curlyhead most of
all.

Just as the little party were leaving Rechberg, Father Clemens was walking along the
moonlit path by the old foot-bridge, smiling, as

he thought of the visit he had made ten days before, at Rechberg, when he had learned the truth in regard to Sepp.

The facts of the case were: Sepp had run away from a hard master, and as the master was a rich farmer of some importance, he did not like to lose a servant for such a reason, so he had complained of Sepp, and put the affair in the hands of the bailiff.

The bailiff had defended Sepp, and told him he had done perfectly right.

Then Father Clemens apppeared, and told the bailiff about Sepp's parents and the two children, and how Sepp had been affected by the loss of his wife.

" He is not a bad fellow," the good man said. " If you will give him a little advice, it may make a good impression on him."

The bailiff promised to do so, and his wife asked further concerning the old people and the children. One thing followed another until the priest told about the lamb which the children had found ; and finally, it came out that it was their Curlyhead. The bailiff and his wife were overjoyed, and charged Father Clemens to bring the children over on Christmas evening, to share in the festival.

That was a great joy to the good priest. He said nothing about the tree, to either the old people or the children; and he smiled again as he thought of their surprise. Now he was going to Joseph's house, that he might see their happy faces on their return.

When he entered the sitting-room, the invalid called out: "I am glad you have come to give us a word of comfort. It is dark already, and the children have to cross the Zillerbach. God forbid that anything should happen to them."

"No, no, grandmother," said the priest cheerfully. "Don't let us complain to-day. There is joy everywhere to-day; and Christ is watching, especially over all children. Nothing will happen to them. Now let us have a good talk together."

Meantime Brownie was flying over the snow, for Sepp felt such a desire to get home again, that he could not go fast enough. He had not been there for six years; and at times, when the thought of home had arisen, he had felt a great heaviness and emptiness, such as he had experienced when Constance died. To get rid of these thoughts Sepp had run still farther away.

But to-day, since he had seen the children, everything seemed different to him; and Stanzeli had brought her mother so vividly before his eyes, and all the peaceful days which he had passed with her and his parents in the home by the willow, that he thought he could not hold out until he should see the house, and father and mother, again. Now the sleigh stopped by the willows. Sepp took the children out, and threw the thick robe over Brownie; then he took the children, one on each side, and entered the room.

He was so overcome that he ran sobbing to the bed, and called out: "Mother! Father! Do not be angry with me, but forgive me. I will certainly do what I can, that you may see better days. I know well that you must have had a hard time; but, God willing, it will be better from this day."

The old people wept for joy, and his mother kept saying: "Ah! Sepp, Sepp, is it indeed possible? I would never have believed that God could so change your heart. I will give

praise and thanks as long as there is any breath
in me." And his father gave his hand, and said:
" It is well, Sepp. All shall be forgiven and
forgotten, and you are welcome! But, tell us
now how you came with the children, and how
things are with you."

First, Sepp had to press the hand of Father
Clemens, who had heard all with a satisfied smile.
Then the parents learned, to their astonishment,
that the bailiff had employed Sepp as a servant,
and had already trusted him with his horse and
sleigh. At New Year's, Hans and Trina wished
to settle for themselves, so there was a servant's
place to fill; and Sepp added delightedly : " And
what a place ! Such a good master, who talks
to me like a father, and good pay besides, and
many an article of clothing through the year,—
that I know from Hans. I have begged the
bailiff, however, not to give me any of my pay,
that I may not mis-spend it ; and, at the end of
the month, you will get it all. I have nothing
to bring now but good will."

" Which is worth everything; and may our
Heavenly Father add his blessing to it," said
Father Clemens.

Seppli, in the meantime, had been wandering up and down, looking for a place to deposit his many treasures. When he saw his opportunity, he crowded up to his grandmother's bed and quickly covered over half of it with his presents; when Stanzeli saw him, she came, too, and covered the other half with hers. It looked like a table at a fair, and the poor woman could only clasp her hands and say: "Is it possible?" But when Sepp brought in the big bundle, and unrolled several beautiful, warm blankets, she was dumb with surprise and gratitude.

Joseph picked up something which rolled out of the blankets, and his eyes shone for joy, for now his only wish was fulfilled. It was a new coffee-mill. Such a joyful Christmas had never been known in the little house by the willows. Sepp held his children as if he could not let them go; and when they saw how their grandparents loved him, they were willing to love him, too.

At last Sepp had to go back to Rechberg; but the bailiff had promised him that he should come every Sunday afternoon to visit his family, so the separation was not to be a long one.

As he was about to drive away, Seppli called after him: " Father, wait.   I must tell you something."

When his father bent down to him he whispered impressively: " Father, when you pass by the chapel, do not forget to go in and pray. God always gives you something, you know; you cannot always see it at the time, but it is sure to come."

Seppli had connected all the joys of the day with the lamb, which he believed God had sent to them in the chapel, in answer to their prayers.

Sepp has proved a trusty and valuable servant at Rechberg. Every Sunday he comes home to Altkirch, bringing a loaf of fresh, white bread for supper.

The delicacies sent by the bailiff's wife, together with the coffee from the new mill, have given new strength to the grandmother, so that she is able to be about the house again, and the little cottage under the willow is so neat and cheerful that Sepp often says to himself, during the week: " Well, home is the best place."

Stanzeli and Seppli often go to play with Lisa, and her brothers, and Curlyhead.

And Lisa, whenever she looks at Curlyhead, thinks, " How happy I am! I will never again conceal a wrong deed in my heart."

BASTI'S SONG IN ALTORF.

WHEN the Christmas holidays were over, and Miss Sunshine's school reopened, each child was allowed to tell what he had enjoyed most during the vacation.

Then Miss Sunshine told them how Christmas was celebrated in different lands. The children were especially pleased with her description of the old English and German custom of sending out children to awaken people, by singing carols under their windows on Christmas morning, and Lawrence remembered that his father had told him that Martin Luther had been famous for his beautiful, silvery voice, when he was a poor boy at school, and used to go from house to house, singing Christmas carols.

When Miss Sunshine promised them that the next story should be about a New Year's carol in Switzerland, everybody tried to get a red letter that very day. And they succeeded.

A big &c. appeared on the blackboard.

While they were all wondering what &c. could possibly mean, Miss Sunshine began the story.

BASTI'S SONG IN ALTORF.

The green fields of Burgeln are very gay in summer, with fragrant grasses and bright flowers.

The little village is surrounded by shady nut-trees, and a busy brook rushes past them, leaping over the stones, in its way.

A foot-path leads along by the brook to an old ivy-covered tower at the end of the village. A very large walnut-tree stands here, in whose shade the traveller pauses to rest, and look up to the high cliffs above, which seem to touch the blue sky.

On the other side of the stream a narrow path goes up the steep mountain-side. Near the bridge stands a little house with a small barn ; higher up is another, and still another, and then, near the top, is the smallest house of all. The door is so low that a man has to stoop to get in, and the shed for the goat is so small that when the goat goes in, there is room for nothing else. The house has only two rooms, and in the summer time the door is left open to let in the light; otherwise, it is quite dark. At the time of our story, a poor woman lived in this house, with her two children, Basti and Franzeli. When the little boy was born, his father looked in the calendar, and found it was St. Sebastian's day; so the child was named Sebastian, which was shortened to Basti. The little girl came on St. Francis's day, and was called Franzeli.

Afra, the mother, was a most diligent, hard-working woman, and after the death of her husband, she still kept her children so tidy, that no one would have guessed that they belonged to the poorest woman in the whole region. Clean clothes were always ready for them on Sunday, and warm stockings were knitted for winter. In summer they wore neither shoes nor stockings.

When these two children came down the mountain hand-in-hand, one man would often say to another,—

"I wonder what Afra does to her children. Mine never look so tidy."

And his neighbor would answer: "Just what I was thinking. I will ask my wife how it is done."

So five years passed away. Basti was now six years old, and Franzeli five; but she was so small and delicate that she looked fully two years younger than her brother.

It had been a cold autumn. Winter set in early, and promised to be a severe one. Snow fell in October, and, in November, Afra's cottage was buried so deep that she could hardly get outside. The children sat in the corner by the stove and never went to the door. Afra went out only when there was not a mouthful of food left in the house. The snow was so deep it was almost impossible for her to get down the mountain, and there was nobody to make a path, except one man who lived above, in whose footprints she tried to step. When she came back she was so weary that she would almost fall down by the way.

But it was not weariness alone which made her sigh when she reached home and sat down to mend her children's clothes. A great anxiety weighed her down, and grew with every day. Often she did not know where the next piece of bread was to come from. She got little work; and for a week at a time she would earn nothing. So she could buy no bread, and the goat's milk would not feed three people. For hours in the night, Afra would lie awake, trying to think how she could earn a little money for the three long winter months before her. She did not sing any more when she put the children to bed; but sat still with her work.

One evening, when the wind was howling outside and shaking the house as if it would overthrow it, Basti's eyes were still wide open; and he lay watching his mother. Suddenly he said: "Why don't you sing any more, mamma?"

"My child," she sighed, "I cannot."

"Have you forgotten the song? I will show you how it goes;" and the child sat up in bed and began to sing: —

> "Now the night is coming on ;
> Darkness everywhere.
> Father, keep thy children still
> In thy tender care."

Basti sang the hymn which he had heard his mother sing so often, with a firm clear voice.

Suddenly a thought came to the poor woman. " Basti, you can help me earn something to buy bread," she said. " Would you like to do it?"

" Yes, yes, I will. Now?" asked the child eagerly, springing out of bed.

" No, no, get into bed again ; see, how cold you are! To-morrow I will teach you a song, which you can sing on New Year's Day, which will soon be here. Then people will give you bread, and perhaps, some nuts."

Basti became so excited at the prospect that he could not sleep, and called out again and again : "Is it morning yet?"

At last he closed his eyes ; but in the morning he woke with the same idea uppermost.

He had to wait till evening, however, for his mother said : " I cannot sing during the day ; I have too much to do."

When it was dark at last, Afra lighted a lamp, and seated herself at the table with a child on each side ; then she took up her knitting, and said : " Listen, Basti ; I will sing the first verse a few times, and then you can try it."

Very soon Basti was able to join in, and suddenly Franzeli began to sing, too.

"That is right, Franzeli," said her mother. "Perhaps you will learn it, too."

When they had sung it together many times the mother said: "Now try it alone, Basti. And will Franzeli help, too?"

The little girl nodded, and began to sing in so clear and silvery a voice that her mother was astonished; and when Basti lost the air, Franzeli sang on, like a bird who knows his melody from beginning to end. It was so sweet that the poor woman thought she could listen forever.

They practised the song every night, and by the end of the week they knew it perfectly. The last day of December had come, and for the last time the children sang the carol to their mother.

These were the words : —

A NEW YEAR'S SONG.

The old year is departing,
  A glad new year draws nigh ;
O, may it bring thee blessings,
  And songs for every sigh.

A large number of children were already out singing New Year Carols.

Cold winter sternly reigneth,
   The earth with ice is bound ;
Yet God is ever working
   Where'er his own are found.

Yet many a little birdling
   For food may hunt in vain;
And children, too, will hunger
   Before the winter's wane.

Now, to all, late or early,
   Much good this year may bring;
God's friends ne'er lack a blessing—
   He helps in everything.

New Year's Day came. Afra went to church early, and then she began to wrap up the children in their warmest things, which were not any too warm.

She wound an old shawl round and round little Franzeli, took the child on her arm, and said; "Now we can go."

Basti went ahead, and struggled manfully through the deep snow until he came to the path by the brook, where he could go beside his mother.

He had so many questions to ask and the time passed so quickly, that they reached Altorf before they knew it.

A large number of children were out already
singing New Year carols. Afra went directly
to the great inn which stood near the old tower.
No singers had yet been here.

She put Franzeli down and sent the children
into the house, while she stood back by the
tower, where she could watch them.

Hand in hand they went inside and began to
sing.

The door of the guest room was opened and
some people called the children in, and praised
them for their singing, and many a bit of bread
and now and then a small coin was put into
their basket. The landlady dropped in a hand-
ful of nuts, saying; "At New Year's time you
must have something to eat with your bread."

The children thanked them all and ran joyfully out to their mother.

They went on to other houses; but so many
different bands of children were trying to sing
at once, that often a man or woman would come
out of the house and say they would rather give
every one of them a loaf of bread than hear
such a noise. Sometimes they had to go away
empty-handed.

At more than one place the mistress of the house came out and called Franzeli and said kindly, "Come, little one, you are nearly frozen. Take this, and then go home."

It was so bitterly cold that Afra herself was almost numb, and Franzeli was shivering so she could scarcely sing. Basti could no longer hold the basket in his hands, they were so stiff; but was obliged to hang it on his arm.

Their mother saw they could endure it no longer, so she took Franzeli again in her arms.

"And you, Basti," she said, "run fast and you will get warm."

When they were at home again, they all sat by the fire to warm their hands and feet, and Basti brought out the basket to see what was in it.

Their mother said the little coins would buy food for many days, and she gave them some bread and the nuts, and they had a merry New Year's Day.

Many sad, anxious days followed, it is true; but at last the long winter was at an end, the warm sun appeared, and the children could go out again.

Poor Afra was no longer obliged to go out and search for wood to warm the little house; but she had worked so hard during the winter, and suffered so many privations, that she had used up all her strength and could not regain it.

She still struggled on, however, in order that the town authorities might not separate her from her children.

Now the long summer days had come. The sun cast a red glow over all the mountain sides where the late hay was spread out to dry.

Afra had gone up with her children to the top of the cliffs, where there was a little spot of land, from which she got hay to feed her goat in the winter. She had cut the grass some days before, and now she bound it up in a great bundle and carried it home on her shoulders.

Little Franzeli held on to her dress, and Basti with his little bundle of hay walked by her side.

They had eaten nothing since morning, except a small bit of bread, and it was now five o'clock.

When Afra took the rest of the loaf out of the cupboard, she was frightened to see how small it was, and she could get no money until the stockings she was knitting were done.

She gave half of the bread to Franzeli and half to Basti, saying; "I know you are very hungry; but you must understand there is nothing more when this is gone. I will knit fast this evening and we will soon have more."

Basti took his piece : but before he bit into it, he looked at his mother, who poured some milk into a little cup for them, and then sat down and laid her head in her hands.

Basti watched her closely.

"Where is your piece?" he asked at last.

"I am not hungry; I do not want anything," replied his mother.

Franzeli came and put a bit of bread into her mouth, but she said, "No, no; eat it yourself; I cannot eat. If I could only go to the doctor in Altorf to-morrow he might help me."

She uttered the last words in a low tone, and suddenly sank back in her chair with closed eyes.

Basti looked at her awhile, and then said, softly: "Come, sister, I know what I will do. But we must be quiet and not wake mamma; she wants to sleep, don't you see?"

The two children went out softly, and started down the mountain side together. As they went along Basti explained: "You see, Franzeli, we are going to Altorf to sing our song again, and we shall get some bread and perhaps some nuts, and we will bring it all to mamma. But can you sing the song still?"

She said she could still sing it, and she was so delighted at the prospect that she walked merrily through the meadows and along the stony street in spite of her bare feet.

They sang as they went, until they found themselves in Altorf. Then they stopped singing, and Basti said: "I know where we must sing first; it is not here."

He went on to the inn, "The Golden Eagle," where their mother had sent them on New Year's Day. But how different it was now! The afternoon sun sent golden beams across the open square in front of the door, and a great noise came from within.

A party of strangers had recently arrived; they were young men in gay-colored caps. They had ordered the great table carried out into the garden, and there they were sitting eating and drinking in great merriment, for they had had a long tramp that day, and were now bent on having a good time.

When Franzeli saw all these young men at the table she stood still in fright; and Basti thought it best to sing at a safe distance. So he began with all his might, in order to be heard above the din.

"Quiet!" suddenly thundered the voice of the large, powerful man who sat at the head of the table. "Quiet! I say; I hear singing. We are having a serenade."

The young men looked around, and when they saw the children, who had placed themselves a little behind the old tower, they beckoned, and called to them, "Come here, come here."

The little ones had stopped singing, and Basti came forward willingly, but he had to drag Franzeli, who was in great terror.

The young man at the head of the table stretched out his long arm and drew Basti nearer, and all the others cried, "Now the song. Barba, let them sing."

"Yes," said the tall man, "your song. Out with it."

Basti sang lustily, and Franzeli's voice chimed in like a silver bell.

> " The old year is departing;
>   The glad New Year draws nigh;
>   Oh, may it bring thee blessings,
>   And songs for every sigh."

"Dear me! We must have got to the other side of the globe; they are celebrating New Year's Day here," cried Barba loudly, which called forth a shout of laughter.

"Be quiet now," said the dark-haired one. "Don't you see how the little Madonna is trembling with fright?"

"You take her, Max," said Barba, "and let us have more of the song."

Max took the child kindly by the hand, and said, "Come, little girl, nobody will harm you."

Franzeli took his hand trustfully, and they sang again : —

> " Cold winter sternly reigneth,
>   The earth with ice is bound;
>   Yet God is ever working,
>   Where'er His own are found."

"I have been spared from the frost to-day," interposed Barba, whose face was glowing with heat.

Another peal of laughter, followed by shouts
of "Go on ! go on ! "

The children sang : —

> " Yet many a little birdling
> For food may hunt in vain;
> And children, too, may hunger
> Before the winter's wane."

" They shall not hunger here," called several
voices, and some plates of goodies were placed
before the children.

But Basti finished his song : —

> " Now to all, late or early,
> Much good this year may bring.
> God's friends ne'er lack a blessing,
> He helps in everything."

A great uproar followed, and every one called,
" That is a good wish ! That will bring us good
luck on our journey ! "

Barba, however, drew Basti to the table, and
put a plate before him heaped with good things,
saying : —

" Now, my boy, go to work, and don't give up
till you have finished it all."

The little boy looked at the plate with longing
eyes, but he did not touch anything. Another

plate had been given to Franzeli, and she was
urged to eat; but, in spite of her great hunger,
after the long walk, she laid the bit of bread
she had taken up back on the plate, when she
saw her brother was not eating.

"What is the matter? Why don't you take
hold, my little fellow? What is your name?"
asked Barba. "Basti," was the answer.

"Good. Well, Basti, what deep thoughts
have taken away your appetite?"

"If I only had a bag!" was all the answer.

"A bag? And what for?"

"Then I would put everything in it, and take
it to mamma. She has had nothing to eat to-
day."

Some of the party immediately cried out for
somebody to bring a bag; others asked him
where his mother lived. When Basti said she
lived up in Burgeln, on the mountain, they were
filled with astonishment, and Barba said, "If
you have come from there, you must be very
hungry. Now confess it, Basti."

"Yes," admitted the boy. "We have not had
much bread to-day, but to-morrow mamma can
finish the stockings, and perhaps we shall have
more."

The child's tale aroused great sympathy. Everybody wanted to do something, — one to get a bag, one to get a man to carry it, — but Barba silenced them all, by saying: —

"First I want to see these children eat all they can, and then we will talk about something else. Now listen, Basti; you must eat all that is on this plate, and the rest your mother shall have."

"All that?" asked Basti.

"All. Now go to work."

Basti grasped his fork, and began to eat with such avidity that the company looked on in amazement.

"Did your mother send you here to sing?" asked Barba.

"No, she went to sleep, because she had eaten nothing, and was tired; and she wants to go and see the doctor," explained Basti. "And so I came here to get something for her when she wakes up. We got some bread the first time we sang here."

Now the students understood how it was that the New Year's Carol had been sung to them, and Barba said: "I propose we should all ac-

company our singers to Burgeln. It will make
a pleasant moonlight excursion."

"And you can have a chance to display your
medical skill," suggested Max.

But when he saw all his friends getting
ready to set out, he cried: "What are you
thinking of? Can that little creature keep
step with us, especially after having been
over the road once to-day? Let mine host
harness his horse, and we will put the little girl, with the basket, in the wagon, and
then go on."

"That's a good idea," observed Barba, with a
glance at the huge basket, which the landlady
had brought for them instead of a bag.

"The best thing of all," continued Barba,
turning to Max, "is for you to remain, and come
with the little Madonna and the basket in the
wagon. We will start off at once, and Basti
shall be guide."

This was agreed upon.

At last they were under way. Barba marched
at the head, and Basti beside him.

Max put Franzeli in the open carriage, and
seated himself beside her, and they drove on in

the beautiful glow, which still lingered in the sky from the setting sun.

Franzeli grew so confidential that she told her companion all about her mother, and Basti and the goat, and what they all did.

In the meantime their mother, at home, awoke from her sleep, but she did not have sufficient strength to get up from the chair. Finally she roused herself a little. It was twilight, and she could not see her children.

She was so tired she could not stir.

"Basti," she called, after some time. "Franzeli, where are you?"

She received no answer. Her anxiety suddenly gave her strength. She rose quickly, and ran out of the little cottage; but nobody was there. She ran around the house, calling the children's names. All was still. Only the sound of the rushing stream reached her ears. A fearful thought came into her mind. She ran to the footpath, and would have rushed wildly down the mountain, but she saw a party of people coming up. They were talking loudly, and she thought she saw them point-

ing up to her little cottage with their alpen-
stocks.

"Oh, God!" she cried, in the greatest terror;
"can it be a message for me?"

She stood as if paralyzed.

"Mother! mother!" she heard all at once;
"we are coming, and you must see what we
are bringing. And the gentlemen are coming
with us, and Franzeli in a carriage with a
horse."

And Basti, rushing on ahead of them all,
tried to tell the whole story before he reached
the top.

Afra's astonishment increased every moment,
as she saw the party of young men, who greeted
her in the friendliest manner, like old acquaint-
ances. Two of them were carrying an immense
basket, on two sticks, put over their shoulders,
and last of all came Franzeli with her companion.

Afra did not know what to think. She gath-
ered from Basti's account the fact that the young
men had shown the children great kindness, and,
indeed, the well-filled basket proved that. She
turned to Barba. As the largest, she considered

him the leader, and she thanked him so heartily that he was much affected.

Overwhelmed with thanks, the students at last took up their line of march down the mountain, and Basti ran to the highest point of the cliff and called as long as he could see them. "Good luck to you, Barba! Good luck to you, Max?" for he had soon learned their names.

When quiet reigned in the little household once more, the children tried to tell their mother everything that had happened since their departure, and Franzeli could hardly find words to express the splendor of it all, especially the driving home in a carriage. But when the great basket was unpacked, and all sorts of good things were taken out, and three whole loaves of white bread remained at the bottom, Basti jumped all over the room in his joy, crying, "Good luck to you, Max! Good luck to you, Barba!"

In the meantime the students were going back to Altorf in a state of high glee. Max had been silent for some time, when he suddenly burst forth with these words: "It is not right yet. No, it is not right. We have only provided means against starvation for a few days and nothing more. What will they do up there in the winter without warm clothes, without food or anything? We have not done enough. We must take up a collection now, to-day, and the landlord can deliver it for us."

"Sir Max," said Barba, "that is a beautiful idea; but it is not practicable. You forget that we are on a journey, that we are far from home, and need something to get us back again. What is there to collect? I will make another proposition. We will found a new league, *the Basti-ana*, — yearly fee, four marks.* We will make our mothers and sisters honorary members, to furnish the necessary frocks and garments for Basti and the little Madonna. Let us collect the fees for the first year as soon as we get home, and invite the honorary members to make their contribution at once."

This plan met with high approval. They re-entered Altorf, seated themselves again at the table in the garden, and there, in the clear moon-light, *the Bastiana* was formally established.

Great was the astonishment of Afra some weeks later, when the post-carrier appeared

* One dollar.

at her house with such an enormous package
that he could hardly get it through the door.
He threw it on the floor, and said as he wiped
his brow: "I cannot imagine what acquaint-
ances you can have in Germany, Afra. Neither
has the postmaster been able to guess who has
sent you such a package from so far away."

"There must be some mistake," replied Afra.

"You can read for yourself," returned the
carrier as he went on his way.

Yes, the name and residence of Afra were
written upon it plainly. With trembling hands
she began to undo the bundle, while the children gazed expectantly at the mysterious object.
All at once the wrappings gave way, and out
fell an astonishing number of little garments,
stockings, and shoes, and in the midst of all
was a heavy roll of silver money.

"From whom does it come? Who can have
sent it?" cried Afra again and again, clasping
her hands in joy.

The mystery was solved when Franzeli
brought her a bit of paper which had fallen on
the floor. On it were these words: —

> "God's friends ne'er lack a blessing,
> He helps in everything."

"That was in the song," cried Basti. "The young men who were at the inn have sent it."

Yes, it could be no one else. An unspeakable joy filled the poor mother's heart as she thought that now she could pass the winter free from anxiety and still keep her children with her.

She was equally surprised next year when a similar package arrived, and the next, and the next, for *the Bastiana* became a permanent institution, and the contributions of clothing and money were sent regularly every year.

As a constant reminder, Afra fastened up on the wall of her room the bit of paper which the students put in the first package : —

> " God's friends ne'er lack a blessing,
> He helps in everything."